SIOBHAN'S BITCHES

RICKY DALE

Published by Ricky Dale
Publishing partner: Paragon Publishing, Rothersthorpe
First published 2023

ISBN 978-1-78792-016-3

Book design, layout and production management by Into Print
www.intoprint.net
+44 (0)1604 832149

A ménage à trois mini saga between
infatuation and love

Readers' Views:
Good, bad and indifferent

☺ *Another virtually true story from the pen of Ricky Dale. This time, however, he bares all regarding his uniquely unconventional family – both in its past and its passion.*

☺ *It's not an epic, it's a behemoth that has the power to shake our perception and touch the soul.*

☺ *A light touch against an epic background – will appeal to almost everybody except the cynical.*

☺ *A gorgeous treat of a story that deserves to be savoured long after you have closed the cover.*

☺ *It is seldom that there comes a novel that can be wholly endorsed as food for quiet humanising thought.*

☺ *The essential humanity of the novel will ensure a very wide appeal.*

☺ *The novel is touching without sentimentality and funny without derision and condescension.*

😐 *The vulgarity of its concept goes without question, however, only the devoutly religious would be shocked.*

😐 *Siobhan came as near to my conception of a harlot, as a soft-centred chocolate!*

☹ *I dislike "Siobhan's Bitches" not because it's salacious but because it is not salacious enough!*

PREFACE

Nigeria never intentionally disappoints or indeed ceases to mystify. Its populace inherits thousands of years of imagination and ingenuity that our so-called modern society has long lost. As a country, it has a spiritual intimacy that, once tasted, you will yearn for more.

Its inborn mystique is not a short-term realism of a treacly charm reserved for soft-headed interlopers because, moreover, it contains enormous unworldly forces. Sorcery, necromancy and juju are somewhat inventive of the Old Testament too.

There is no question that Nigeria will take your identity and present you with its own identity in return – and you will be so obliged that it has done so too! As stealthy as a female mosquito who inaudibly transmits to its quarry; the infection it gives will live on in your body and soul for the rest of your days – of that you can be sure!

At not such a deep level, there is an endearing quality to laying on top of your bunk in the evening, listening to those gospel crickets, infused with the hazy dreamy background of drum beats – even the redolent burning of the day's latrines can have an almost singular appeal.

Perhaps you may deem all of this sentimental speculation as being more schmalz. However, read on, steep yourself into the incidental indoctrination of a lady from Donnybrook and two brothers from Devonshire – and then you decide!

A veteran colonist would most probably dismiss 'emotionally dependent active chemical forces' as being irrelevant to Nigerian lore and that the 'threesome' that I aforementioned simply 'went bush' – maybe so!!

A civil war can almost certainly guarantee that prudence comes first, even if a person is unenthusiastic about losing their home. Us being shot at was our slam bang finale to packing and boarding the SS Calabar at Lagos docks, bound for Blighty in 12 hours. At Sierra Leone a supplemental group of passengers came on board, including an Irish lady named 'Siobhan'.

She was hokey; she was gorgeously manipulative and cunning; she was just an exhilarating prodigal synthesis of mirth and pleasure come true ... and a decade or so our senior too!

From that day onwards we were our *ménage à trois* and nothing on earth could ever come between us!

INTRODUCTION

All points of view and perspectives contained in this novel have an out and out claim to an integrity of sorts. The veracity of every word and situation is what I have tried to engender in my writing and thereby in spirit in you, my reader. Fundamentally, this novel is not a long and rambling account of lubricious protagonists who fuck together; nor is it a confused and confusing ambiguously indiscriminate orgy per se. It is, however, both an unwittingly and powerful love story between a group of three people – instead of two. Let's be honest – to be utterly 'smitten' is not necessarily a gender led pursuit in any event!

Ricky Dale

To : Mark & Anne ; Dr. Kim ; Christelle & Melody ; Dianne ;
and not least ; Lee .

CONTENTS

Part 1

AFRO-ENGLISH BEATS

A silver trumpet sounds the alarm at Kano airport and maintenance workers scurry like exuberant confused beetles off the cool tarmacked runway. The Hausa trumpeter looks majestically tall and slim in his long snowy white gown; which sweeps down from his pronounced shoulders to the laterite ground below. This is unquestionably his brief moment of timed authority and he confidently makes the very most of it – indeed, blowing a somewhat tuneful fanfare from an eight-foot-long trumpet, is no mean feat.

For the BOAC Argonaut which had left London two days ago, its journey was nearly over. However, the second leg of our journey by West African Airways – from Kano to Lagos – was about to begin. It could be argued that we all should have perished yesterday afternoon on some unyielding sand dune in the Sahara; but for providence and Captain L Ives, it all just became another entry in my nifty journal! I remember the address system advising that there had been a slight hitch and that we would be returning to Tripoli.

Even to this day I am uncertain of all the technicalities of what exactly the cause was. Suffice to say that three out of our four propellors were no longer functioning, and that we were losing altitude at a rate of knots.

The Chief Steward and Stewardess were continuously leaning across the passengers and rubber-necking through the small portholes with kind of lightweight hatchets. I remember our cabin crew commenting that the Bedouin were conspicuously visible, bivouacked below. With regard to us passengers, we all seemed extremely accepting of our lot! There wasn't an iota of tizzyness among us. My dear brother Mike spotted what we assumed were the lights of Tripoli in the near distance. The hyperactive harum-scarum crew were quick to echo this and the aircraft began its unconventional descent – like a stone with sheer exhaustion!

As the tarmac came up to greet us, Mike and I seems incapable of uttering a single word, but the look we gave each other said it all – we inwardly knew that in the order of importance, us two brothers took precedence. The enormous aircraft actually bounced across the runway with an almost elasticated airworthiness. As the plane came to a halt two stewardesses had unfastened one of the emergency doors and without hesitation had leapt out onto the runway. I'd seized hold of my brother's hand and Mike and I were the next to debark; having shin-kicked a steward who had other ideas!

Mike and I just gathered up our indiscretions and ran like blooming blue murder toward the spired control tower and safety. We could hear the one remaining engine almost objectively continuously roaring along with a ruckus of fellow travellers who all seemed to be following us! Mike summed up superbly our descent from the fuselage door, saying "we were like blind ants in an engineering museum: vulnerable, inoffensive and innocently transparent among the cylinders and miasma of blue gas". Mike always seemed to find an irony that penetrates the philogyny and ontogeny of a situation! As we reached the control tower, at least fifty arms wrapped – around us – it was really a compassionate moment, although I'd have rather they hadn't scrunched my hair!

Inside of me was a judge who was thoroughly pissed off with BOAC's monkey tricks – not Captain L Ives you understand; he had saved the day. However, the unprofessional antics of the flight crew put me in mind of apathy at its worst. However, I felt more inclined to forgive after BOAC raised their game and accommodated us in a sloaney chic hotel overnight. If memory serves it was called 'Dema-Hara', Arabic I imagine! Mike and I only ever had landladies in the past. I remember us now laying on our king-size beds that evening, scotch and water gratis and blowing vague circles of smoke into the air-conditioned suite; both of us incapable of uttering a single word.

Within 24 hours we were in the air again heading toward Kano and then our final destination Lagos. The airport at Lagos was little more than a couple of runways with a low, shed-like structure of about three rooms housing customs inspection, ticket counter, car rental and waiting room. Mom and Dad were waiting patiently to meet us by the custom shed.

I can't remember my parents having many close friends – perhaps one or two and the cleaning lady who helped out when we were youngsters. However, along with our parents there seems to be the whole European contingent waiting there to express their commiserations! It was a really hot Wednesday afternoon in the middle of May and much too hot to stay outside. After all of the obligatory hugs we realised that the ground crew had no intention of removing our baggage from the aircraft. I struck up a conversation with a big husky blond man in his thirties whose luggage had arrived. "You won't ever get your luggage, not unless you 'dash' them first. Either pay 'em or check back in to the aircraft and continue flying – this time I'd take a parachute" he added laughing; welcome to Nigeria!!

It's curious how it's often the more insignificant events that you tend to recall upon your first arrival upon unfamiliar soil – perhaps even more so than a grim event. Resting under my mosquito net and meandering over the past 24 hours, it wasn't the near death happening that focused my thoughts, in contrast it was the bundles of newspapers being thrown out of the aircraft to supposedly lighten the load. Most likely The Times and Telegraph for expatriates who don't mind reading yesterday's papers at today's breakfast table. For the many missionaries, soldiers and traders the hurried along newspapers from Blighty were a piece of home. However, Ibadan was to be our home for the unforeseeable future, more so than we ever could have envisaged. It was for the most part a Yoruba township; although there was an influx of Ibo too, everyone got on really well nevertheless.

Spending your first few days in Nigeria could be both an endearing and irritating participation in head-on acquiescing. Inasmuch that there are more than enough groovy little insects who are not bashful in getting to know you! For example, the simple lighting of a kerosene oil lamp is a red flag to mosquitoes, beetles, mantises, fireflies, sausage ants, dauber wasps and all of their compassionate confederates! I recall a cute little night-lizard whose body is completely translucent; it was quite engaging to watch the insects it gorged on going down its belly!

Mike and I enjoyed spending time out at a British Army camp. Although the camp was in the back of beyond, the C-in-C had allowed us to utilise a decommissioned four-wheel drive which was "excess to requirements". Once or twice a week they'd show a movie at the camp. The screen consisted of a ten-foot by ten-foot whitewash wall – it was a walkover rout for four-legged reptiles and the such. I recall watching "Thunder Road" one evening. The superb Robert Mitchum as a Kentucky bootlegger, and breath-taking Keely Smith his lady love with an enormous lizard on her backside. The camp also boasted a second to none pool table – problem being was that the lamplight attracted these irregular shaped 'sausage' flies. Once they'd shed their wings, they would run around willy-nilly all over the green turf! We couldn't believe good fortune, when Paul Newman's "The Hustler" unexpectedly became our Friday night viewing. Newman was electrifying – Mike even wanted to change his name to Eddie Felson; and he wasn't kidding either!

Seems to me that 'stars' such as Brando and Palance gave us the fallacious belief we needed – to be like them! Our Dad wasn't someone who we recognised as a person we wanted to be like. He belonged to Mom and her to him and Mike and I were separate to requirements. It was intended that Mike and I remain in the UK, with all we still had our home and a small income to live on as well. Apparently, it was customary among other colonial parents to abandon their offspring in a UK boarding school. I was never struck by that idea in any event, but Mom put it more bluntly: "you are most likely to cop National Service Ricky, but Mike would risk being buggered by those older boys in boarding school for certain".

I guess that our choice to leave the UK made it all straightforward. Mom and Dad's decision had been made for them, and joining the military or risk being buggered was a no-brainer! From the onset us kids fell in love with our new Nigerian home. Mike kind of adopted the persona of Johnny Weissmuller – best known as the longest-serving Tarzan – and I (near fully grown) became Stewart (Bhowani Junction) Granger; with tree houses to boot! We both got over malaria and Dengue early on in our African adventure and the fact that a decade ago this region was known as "white man's graveyard", didn't faze us in the slightest.

I guess in our own fashion us kids loved our parents but only inasmuch that it was appropriate for us to do so.

Even at our early age we were fully aware that they were both a little wacko. By profession our father was a civil engineer – roads and bridges were his thing. By nature he was something of a wonderlistic fool. Mom, on the other hand, had been blessed with the "smarts"! She was Devon farming stock and possessed a kind of canniness that only born and bred country folk are equipped with. Mom wasn't a pregnant and barefoot wimpy female by any stretch!

Oftentimes Nigeria can weave its irrefutable magnetism into a person's psyche. The Irish call it "pishogue". The English call it "going bush"! Sorcery or forthright scummy, not too much time had ticked by before our Dad was seeking the company of at least two Nigerian mammys; and our Mom was enthralling a selection of freshmen from the University College Hospital.

The self in us lived, and it wasn't that long before our family became totally disconnected from our previous lives in England. Perhaps we had become more urbanised and worldly-wise. Kind of less constricted and somewhat more innovatory than before. Even though I had always been a studious kid, I had outgrown paintbrushes and crayons. Even Mike had converted to a grown-up overnight. Just one of the innumerable quirks that I adored about Nigerian culture, is the way in which a person's age bears little or no significance to the estimation of said person. For example, in Britain we penalise the young by virtue of their age and we punish the elderly as being past their sell by date. In Nigeria a person is either a 'big man' or a 'little man' and never the twain shall meet! And women; they already have the whole palindrome sussed and just snap to it!

Having such a libertine father and lascivious mother, Mike and I were self-sufficient steely kids, caught somewhere between being 'big' and 'little' ad nauseam. Another quirkiness that I found endearing was the Nigerian habit of referring to all colonialists as 'European'. I distinctly recall an American contractor getting unfathomably angry over this mention that he was a 'European'. "I'm a god-damned American" he replied. "No sir, you are a European!" was his proponent's critical comeback.

The colonialist, whether European or otherwise, came primarily for exploration or exploitation. Indeed, the slave trade had reached its peak in the eighteenth century. And then into the nineteenth century there came folks with somewhat more altruistic motives. All wishing to extend 'their' doctrines and dogma to the mismatched Nigerian tribes. This inappropriately named 'knowledge and morality' became what the writer refers to as Nigeria's dissolution. It was only in the twentieth century, after the savagery of two world wars that a profound pessimism combined with pragmatic considerations, led many European powers to accept the vacuous inevitability of decolonisation now that the rapacious rape was decisively at an end.

Mike and I were aware of the stain from the onset, it was as though an innate shrewdness had incredulously cautioned us. When you are at one with an entity it empowers you to feel its pain. We knew that our time had materialised to bid farewell to these malaise shores. Mom and Dad had already made their plans to move on. They had completed some 54 months in Nigeria and were becoming fidgety in any event. It transpired that The Hudson Bay Company in Canada had headhunted him. Mom said that the contradictory topography was appealingly enticing.

Mike and I were of the age now that allowed us an equal say into whether or not we wished to accompany our parents. We opted to remain in Nigeria for a few months and then return to Blighty to dip our toes, so to speak! Our off the wall views didn't ever irritate our parents; in fact, they were understanding. Mom would sometimes cry a little and Dad often ranted but, by and large, we all got on with our own lives!

Etiquette was an overriding factor for colonists in 1950's Nigeria, and being washed scrubbed and dressed correctly for our evening meal was an expectancy. At 7pm sharp, on the dot, Mom, Dad and us kids sat around the rococo dining table and all was right in the world after Mom rang her tiny brass bell; which signalled service. Dad and us kids invariably wore our whites (without tie). Mom often favoured a long loose kaftan (not garish) and always wore a string of oyster pearls draping nonchalantly from her slim neck. Gabrial and Christopher our 'house boys' were also suitably dressed in their khaki shorts and shirts. After attending table their duties were finished for the day.

Oftentimes Mom placed a blushing hibiscus flower in the centre of the table. The flowers would have been picked in the early morning, whilst cool. By placing them in the fridge they remained white until evening when they slowly metamorphosed to ruby red.

I mentioned about Gabrial and Christopher being our 'house boys'; this was a kind of disrespectful term used by Europeans. More accurately they were our friends – and Housa too; he tended the grass and flower beds. They all resided with their wives and children in a brick-built commune at the uppermost point of our main compound. It wasn't a shanty town; each family had their separate accommodation with running water and electricity relayed from our bungalow. The shower room was enormous and consisted of a dozen or so showers with breeze block-built seats under them. There wasn't a roof, the shower room was completely open to the sky. Mike had always been a hellacious kid and chose to scale the eight-foot-high wall and sit there on the parapet eyeballing Housa partake of a shower.

"Gee whizz, you've got a big dipper Housa"

"Yes, master Michael, it is a very big pinnip"

Housa, of course, was referring to his penis, however, in his pidgin English, it became translated as 'pinnip'! Mike hadn't heard of that part of the male anatomy being referred to as either 'pinnip' or indeed 'penis' and, therefore, when explaining to us all around the dinner table, Mom and Dad assumed that Housa had perhaps bought another dog called 'pinnip', and it was big!

'Baby' was our pet goat. She had been an endearing companion of our family life since we brought her home from the local market some four years ago. When we went out for rides in the car or indeed to the beach, Baby would come along too. Mom was truly perturbed leaving Baby behind – she felt she couldn't trust us kids with the responsibility of looking after Baby. That, and the likely fact that in the event Baby were to slip out of our safe compound she would be caught and chomped up by the locals.

It was the way in which Mike had enquired if anyone had seen Baby that evening and Mom had validated Mike's query by dispassionately gesturing toward our dinner plates. Mom assured us all that she had killed Baby humanely and, in the same breath, she restoratively added how it was a shame and wasteful not to have used up all that meat! As it happened, many years later Mom passed away slightly before Dad. I swear if Dad had passed away first, she'd have made a fricassee of him! Perhaps being raised on a Devonshire farm, together with wartime rationing helps to justify Mom's commonsense pragmatism!

Several days later Mom and Dad headed back to Blighty for a short period before pushing on to Canada. Mike and I kind of became orphans of own making in that seriously copious-sized bungalow. It had been constructed over a decade and a half ago for the first British regional governor: 'The Representative of the British Crown in a Commonwealth State' – so to speak! The residence became available after said governor was shipped back to England. An unconfirmed rumour had him catching dengue; however, tittle-tattle says he had been caught significantly misappropriating dash! Mom and Dad had purchased the property for a very small sum of money, after it had stood empty longer than was expected. And now it all belonged to us; lock, stock and barrel. Although it wasn't really an investment per se, inasmuch that with the country's independence looming, many Europeans were grabbing their chattels and heading home. For Mike and I, Nigeria was the only home that we could bring to mind in an impassioned way and, for that reason, we weren't going anywhere soon. With all that in mind, we decided to have a kind of pow-wow with our former 'house boys' for the purpose of establishing a more suitable living arrangement. The bungalow was ample enough to accommodate all of us, and the upshot was they moved out of their not so salubrious quarters and into the former governor's home! After a shake of hands, the other formalities were incidental.

Apart from Housa who had a full-time responsibility keeping the compound at moderately lengthened, the remainder of our group required work! It was not the big deal that we had anticipated it might be. We got Gabrial and Christopher employed to a wealthy Nigerian family who lived close by and us kids found some well paid jobs with West African Airways administrative department.

Everything seemed settled: Nigeria and its people, a microcosm of different families – Yoruba, Ibo, Hausa, Kanuri and us; me and Mike! We all made up a teeming population of a country as old as pre-history and as new as a nation; which sadly achieved its independence on October 1st 1960! Independence was not the negation of goodness as we thought it might be, however it was the replacement of a positive by a negative and we were part of the pretence!

Mike's most treasured possession was an outworn Chevy tipper truck which he had fortuitously procured from the neighbourhood witch doctor. Whether verifiable or just pure supposition, Mike had convinced him (the witch doctor) that he (Mike) was an English sorcerer (wizard) who had magical powers to not only foresee the future but also to liaise with departed souls. If you could have known Mike in those days the probability is that you might give credence to bullshit too. His knowledge of wands, cups and pentacles combined with his beguiling long blond hair and piercing blue eyes – he could make a Mormon doubt Joseph Smith. Oftentimes he would present his newly acquired friend a gift. I recall Mike contributing a mountainous basket of kola nuts[1] – our compound was an orchard of kola trees.

My reader is forgiven for finding it difficult to take on board precisely what life was like during these bedazzling decadent decades. For example, we had no television – couldn't even anticipate or envisage what such a thing would be like. We did have a radio of sorts, however it had to be tuned with a screwdriver and only worked on automobile batteries. And we did have a record player with four Chuck Berry singles, one Crosby and one Doris

---

1 Kola nuts come from a big tree in the Western part of Nigeria – the Yoruba land. They are tropical evergreens. The significance of them is both cultural and medicinal. They contain serious caffeine and mashed together can have quite an effect on a person's receptiveness!

Day. They were all somewhat wavy from continuous use.

It was an established essential to bathe once or twice daily. With water and electricity becoming susceptible to cuts – oftentimes for a period of seven days – we set out our own back-up plan. 'Ocean River' was unobtrusively located exactly five miles from our bungalow. Our Dad had discovered it whilst surveying the hinterland. Sheltered by trees and thick forests, even some local folks were unaware of its outlandish existence. It was kind of like a hugely welcoming rocky pool, where glowing volumes of water flowed in from a steep slope and spilled out at the other end. This was our oasis – it gave a whole new connotation to the literal meaning of having a bath!

Whensoever necessity dictated, we'd all pile into Mike's forlorn Chevy and hightail across to Ocean River. Gabrial and Christopher reckoned on one wife each as being plenty adequate, however Housa rivalled them by having three wives and five children too! Mike's tipper catered for the complement!

Carbolic disinfectant soap and an immeasurable number of sponges from Lagos Bay[2] were our key essentials; and the kids would bring along several inflatable inner tubes. Mike, me and our 'house boys' would strip down to our underpants, inevitably Housa et al had no doubts about letting it all hang out! Our

---

2 We'd purchase these defunct invertebrates from the local market for 1p each, and they were humongous in size too.

hearty ablutions weren't in any respect timed, but by the hour that it began to get dimsicle we were strolling back through the bush to Mike's truck. There was never a need to towel dry ourselves, and the journey home with the cool air entrenching us was heavenly. Great and simple time they were ours – misunderstanding, mistakes, accidents and even so-called disasters; Mike and I owned them, for better or for worse!

We had unquestionably forged an emotional alliance with this illustrious country and yet failed to realise just how vulnerable that had made us and how fragile its greatness was becoming. Our Nigeria was growing darker, like the blood of a magnificent bull gushing in torrents of tar upon the slabs of abattoiral hideousness. Our lives of opulence were becoming a sob. Scissors were advancing, serenely and deviously across mountains, valleys and bushland; over waters and across thought. The narrowness of time had carried us to the knife's edge and beyond the privilege that had guided us here.

The Nigerian army was completely unready for war. It had had no training as such on an operation level, and was primarily an internal security force – that's all. The same problems also affected the Biafran army and consequently when the war began in the early hours of July 6th 1967, the whole litany of events resulted in the loss of thousands of troops and mass killings of entire populations!

Britain sat on its hands as usual and it was not until Nigerian forces captured the oil terminal at Bonny Island that our British Prime Minister Harold Wilson decided to back Nigeria with military aid.

Mike and I watched as efforts to relieve the Biafran people were thwarted by the desire of Nigeria to pursue unconditional victory. After one too many stones and handfuls of laterite had been hurled at our vehicle, we agreed to hightail it on to pastures new. All in all, our country had been fallaciously dismembered. Puts me in mind of a book my grandma had sent me; a cloaked skeleton holding a large scythe was on the sleeve!

The British Ambassador in Lagos acquired us a first-class berth on the SS Calabar and, within several days, we were unexpectedly bidding farewell to our beloved friends Gabrial and Christopher. Housa had joined the army some weeks previously. Leaving them behind seemed like a heinous crime. As the Calabar ploughed its route past the sands of Tarqua Bay and out into the vast ocean proper, Mike and I shared an identical silence. For the larger number of passengers, it was homeward bound – for us kids it was as though we were deserting our home, leaving it high and dry!

I Sing of Change

Niyi Osundare – born March 12th 1947, Ikere-Ekita, Nigeria

I sing
Of the beauty of Athens
Without its slaves

Of a world free
Of kings and queens
And other remnants
Of an arbitrary past.

Of earth
With no
Sharp north
Or deep south.
Without blind curtains
Or iron walls.

Of the end
Of warlords and armouries
And prisons of hate and fear

Of deserts treeing
And fruiting
After the quickening rains

Of the sun radiating ignorance
And the stars informing
Of nights unknowing

I sing of a world reshaped

W. B. Yeats – born Dublin, 1865

Sing on:

Somewhere, at some new moon.
We'll learn that sleeping is not death;
Hearing the whole earth change its tune.

Part 2

MÉNAGE À TROIS

After about three days into the voyage, we docked at Sierra Leone to take on more passengers and a supplementary crew. Back on the high seas again we noticed a few new faces around deck including a strikingly handsome woman who was partaking of tea and cakes with the purser. He beckoned us over to their table and after some informal introductions, politely insisted that we all join him at the captain's table for dinner that evening.

I guess that evening was a life changer; it was one of those curious occasions that whilst doing absolutely nothing, we felt free to undertake everything. A miraculously short time that convinces a person that even if tomorrow never comes they will have found forever today. Everyone should sit at the captain's table at some point in their lives!

Somewhere between hors d'oeuvres and the main course Siobhan made her appearance. The speculation over who would occupy the reserved seat had been solved! An affectionate kiss on the cheek for the captain, as we all stood whilst she serenely seated. From that moment on, it almost felt as though we were Siobhan's blind date. Indeed that, maybe, it was us who had arrived somewhat late. In fact, it was the crucial point where our lives had ended and that the dreams that were to become the rest of our lives began. When, on most occasions, it is only necessary to 'share' with a total stranger some gentle conversation – on this occasion it was just not enough by far!

The air seemed filled with songs – God's beauty unfolded before our eyes. Seems to me I'd been used to dating girls with sweatshirts or rough warm woolly sweaters – her evening dress, the severe nakedness of her back. It was about time I learned that the past can be changed, if you know what you want! This kind of sureness comes only once in a lifetime. A kind of sureness that you want to share – you need to share. I recall many years later, Mike heartening me with his Alice in Wonderland blending of: "We kept her in the family Ricky; that's what needed to be done and that's what is really central to the three of us – nothing more or less!"

Without asking for her permission, Mike offered Siobhan his hand and kind of pragmatically coaxed her onto the dance floor. Mike was an unashamed 'gyrator' and he admittedly knew it! Fortunately, the combo had exhausted their middle-of-the-road repertoire during dinner and had begun to settle into some entertaining swing numbers. Mike and I were on the same page when it came to musicality – although in application he was a more adaptable guitarist whereas my plucking and strumming were more suited for a lively hoedown! As time would tell when it came to like-mindedness Siobhan, Mike and I were appropriate bedfellows, inasmuch that her musicality – like sex – contained an abundance of variety!

Having spent much of our recreational time practicing cuckoldry with various contractors' wives in the back seat of their vehicles, it was kind of nice to upgrade. Not just yet with Siobhan though. She was some 15 years our senior and had a cagey Irish nose for what was going on in our pants! Until she was ready, she chose to remain as celibate as a grinning priest of stinginess. On the other hand, Mike and I were not unlike two high school fans with 40 cents to buy a 50-cent sundae split – cherries and banana! From this moment on it was all about waiting and baiting for us two would be Di Maggio's. Siobhan would call the shots if and when she deemed her presence was appropriately appreciated and not before.

By all accounts Siobhan's marriage had long been on the edge. She told us later that we hadn't worsened it – we'd just added some self-certification. In bar-rooms, dining rooms, school rooms, hotel rooms, waiting rooms and even whores' rooms. Mike and I would not only give her past relationship some 'self-certification' but also, we would profoundly shut it down completely – of this there was no doubt!

By the time that the Callabar docked at Tilbury, Mike and I were pretty much shagged-out! It's incredible how a constitutional meander around the ship's circumference each day can become shockingly wearisome! Oftentimes Siobhan would join us – I always thought that in the morning her legs looked even longer – Mike remarked that he thought so too. When you share the significant things, three is never going to be a crowd – and it's what loving brothers should do in any event.

As Mike and I had no particular place to go, Siobhan offered to put us up at her folk's house in nearby Gravesend.

Siobhan – At First Sight

Should we speak unthinkingly,
Rashly, outwardly,
Or look, wordlessly?

Move determinedly
Or wait expectantly?
She sighs slightly.

We turn anxiously
She sits quietly
Smiling distantly.

Either lie, passionately,
Or not lie, fruitlessly?
We pause, two-mindedly.

To love wishfully,
Blindly, entirely,
Self-transformingly;

Or to stay truthfully
In doubt, wistfully
Doomed to reality?

Her face, held beautifully,
Looks at us questioningly,
We watch her, wonderingly.

To love recklessly,
Hazarding certainty
Losing identity;

Or to feel warily –
Vows made conditionally,
Words weighed carefully,

She looks up suddenly,
Her eyes speaking clearly
Our thoughts, completely

Poised unbelievably,
We touch magically,
And light strikes, blindingly

Siobhan's folks lived in a somewhat dejected Victorian terraced house just abutting Gravesend park. Her elderly Mom welcomed Mike and me as though we were the second coming. Her Dad scarcely spoke at all; instead, he jiggled his backside on the wicker chair and reproachfully continued reading his newspaper.

For supper, Siobhan's Mom had baked an enormous pastry and vegetable pie – put me in mind of Desperate Dan's cow pie in The Dandy! Shortly after we had all eaten, a visitor arrived carrying a compact leather suitcase – this intrusion was Mom's cue to clear us and the dirty dishes away without delay. There is not a lot I can say about our evening visitor except for his Donald

Duck eyes (very much aware) and the barrel of a revolver tucked into the side of his trouser belt.

It seems to me, that in many respects our simple lives in Nigeria had seemingly served to protect us from the phenomenal badness that was happening elsewhere in the world. Inasmuch we didn't often get the opportunity to buy a newspaper and very rarely ever listened to a radio broadcast. I guess that could be the reason why when Siobhan let it slip that her grizzled old Dad was a head honcho in the Irish Republican Army it really did nothing to impress us colonials. Except perhaps to suggest there might be a parallel between Duck Eyes, the English army and that revolver?

It had never occurred to us that the IRA – who we began to become more acquainted with – was a paramilitary organisation who favoured guerrilla warfare against British rule in Ireland. We had known many bumptious egotistic army types in Nigeria, but we put up with their holier than thou attitude. We watched movies and played snooker at their camp, so no great problems! I guess that what concerned Mike and I, at this particular moment in time, was the contents of 'Donald Duck's' small leather suitcase – did it contain bicycle parts or something more ominous in nature!? "You won't be alluding to my visit here tonight, will you boys" he hissed. A bizarre thing happens when a stranger asks a question like that – it's as though the transparent matter that hides the meaning of his words has been meticulously peeled off and made each blank word extremely visible! Metaphorically speaking we could feel the cold steel of a gun barrel chillingly licking our necks and the subtle command to remain shushed was as clear as shrapnel!

To all intents and purposes Mike and I were bearers of an affiliation from a very different world and the sensation of being here, in England, in thus chilly uncomfortable parlour room – where even the coal fire in the grate seemed somewhat compromised – was not something we were accustomed to or indeed could become accustomed to in time. I've heard it said that the year in which a person dies can oftentimes present itself as the best year of their life. That being the case, it was not that reassuring to agree that the year just gone had been pretty good to Mike and I. Returning to England though was a difficult connection for us to come to terms with. In many respects our arrival was beginning to feel like we were edging into an incompatible alien country, not necessarily drawn on any impalpable map – and that evolution had somehow put us on a knife's edge of something ugly that we didn't entirely understand.

With nowhere to go when we arrived in England, it was Siobhan's testimonial that had allowed us access and acceptance into this clammy surreptitious powerhouse here on Edin Street. She had become everything towards which all of our senses propelled us. The foolhardy fantasy that her legs always looked longer in the early morning, and that strawberries would condense in her kisses: versus the Irish guy with his binoculars and foldaway rifle barrel. They are both not entirely and insignificant point of reference!

Sometime, somewhere in a particular location in the

universe, perhaps the Lord would consider creating for Mike and I, three Siobhans – one each for us guys, and a separate one who is not so scary!

It was more than Irish folklore that dictated Siobhan had a ground floor bedroom adjacent to her parents' room. On the other hand, Mike and I were assigned to a large attic room on a top floor landing. For the time being, closeness of a reciprocal nature had been replaced by frustration and insomnia. It seems to me that this form of safe sex was for our well-being. Mike and I had become the proverbial template of self-control whenever Siobhan's rather indomitable family and friends were in attendance, which they invariably were. It was somewhat an arduous task having a get-together with coldly determined partisans with whom we had little in common.

At our first meeting we thought that Martin Cahill and his younger sibling John, were alright, down to earth sort of guys. We liked the account they had told us regarding their father being a lighthouse keeper on Ireland's Atlantic coast – kind of romanticised our perception of the emerald isle. Also, the similarity of them being brothers too. Apparently, they had originally come from Dublin's south side, but had been taken in by Siobhan's parents after the Oblates of Mary Immaculate had found them homeless. Mike and I had always been together and it had been a long time since we had any 'outsiders' as friends. For a while we enjoyed the novelty.

Looking back on our futile relationship with the Cahills from a hindsight perspective, it was obvious that their luck would eventually run its course. Inasmuch that after we had moved on, they became involved in all sorts of shenanigans, which culminated in Martin being shot. Apparently, a motorcyclist armed with a .357 magnum revolver shot him at point-blank range. Rumour suggests that Cahill was executed by the Provisional Irish Republican Army for collaborating with the loyalist paramilitaries of the Ulster Volunteer Force; it's all double Dutch to me!

Someone's coming to confession who finds it more and more difficult to meditate – that's how we were beginning to feel. More and more we were finding it harder to use human speech to reply "no, we don't want to join you boyo's". It was becoming a difficult household to live in. Inasmuch that Siobhan's mother's watchful eye was never far removed, Mike, me and Siobhan took turns in the garden shed and then would sneak back into the house like it really doesn't matter – but it did! Just being together for as many minutes, hours, days or years was everything that we'll ever need, as long as we are 'we'!

Mike and I had broken into our Nigerian savings and it was blatantly obvious that our 'life of Riley' – no pun intended – had runs its course. For domestic and financial considerations, it was time to seek pastures new. But it was more so than that: between error and truth, between instinct and rationality, between the dead brother and the live brother – and Siobhan too; her fullness was difficult to dislodge from reality. Utterly shameless, like reptiles with phosphorescent blood in their veins, we snuck out of the house in the early hours of Sunday morning. As we approached dank Gravesend railway station, a far-off thunder of some last downpour resounded like a memory of the summer just past. We had decided to head to Devon where we had been born – but not bred – long before our father put his wanderlust into practice!

"Were you going to leave without a single goodbye kiss?" It was our Siobhan lugging an overfilled suitcase along the empty platform toward us. "I am coming too" and with that perfect reassurance we all hugged like the exuberant lovers of the heart we had become. It was as though our child's psyche had overruled our adult's logic and was screaming in unison: "please never go away, this is the life we choose, don't allow conformity to spoil it".

It seemed like a lifetime since Mike and I had sadly left our childhood home in the endearing town of Torquay. Situated in the captivating county of Devon, England. When the train came to a halt at Torquay railway station, everything seemed to be just the way we had left it – even the fall of leaves on the platform was still waiting patiently to be swept. The location of the train station is directly on the lengthy seafront and conveniently adjacent the appropriately named 'Grand Hotel'. This huge edifice of a building is not unlike an imitation French chateau. We wanted to let Siobhan see how debonair our home looked, and so agreed to stroll the length of the seafront around to the harbourside. The promenade where the bathers hung out looked more elegant than we taken note of when we were kids. Mike remarked how strange it was that none of the bathers wore bathing caps as they used to. Odd how it's sometimes the little things that draw a person's attention when they've been away.

Siobhan was fairly certain that some friends of the family had recently settled in Torquay. And so, with that thought in mind and the hope that they would agree to put us up for a few nights, we began to scan the local telephone directory. Siobhan was always rescuing us, like a big sister ... not hardly!!

We were all getting hungry, and I remembered that close by was an Addison café where Mom had shared a 'cream tea' with us kids years ago. I should point out that 'cream teas' are a favourite treat for locals and visitors alike! Afterwards we all bundled into a rakish looking taxicab and headed to Siobhan's friend's abode in the curiously named 'Pennsylvania Road'. From the outside we could detect the coloured lights of a Christmas tree radiating through the grubby sash window – a freakish kind of September, no doubt! All of the houses in this street were predominantly identical Edwardian terraces. Daubed upon the molasses-coloured front door was a sign reading "Nothing opposes us". Unprepared, even now – it seemed to be one of those ominous junctures in life where a person (or persons) may feel like running away from whatever privilege had brought them here in the beginning! Our hosts Kenneth and Keith Littlejohn were extremely cordial, and Jack Daniels on ice promptly waylaid the contrition of our fears that September evening.

The interior of their home was not atypical of a house of that year. It was more consistent with an open-plan dormitory in an institution; inasmuch there were no corridors or passageways linking the rooms. Access to each floor was via a broad set of stairs that seemed to stand-alone. Our huge bedroom on the top floor was private only by the virtue that it appropriated the entire floor. The sitting room or front parlour reminded me of a hotel or theatre foyer or reception area. It was filled with reclining armchairs, all styleless! "I acquired them in a job lot from a blind Jew" Kenneth quipped. I remember thinking that all we required was a megaphone to speak to one another.

I guess Kenneth and Keith could sense our befuddlement and so endeavoured to throw some light on: "we lead a kind of 'Walter Mitty' type of life" Kenneth confessed merrily. Keith added: it's the British Ministry of Defence who mediates at our confessions on a Sunday, not a priest! Kenneth laughed aloud like he was evaluating the indelible disrepair of their arduous destiny. He used a profanity "we work for f***ing shop assistants who cannot differentiate between petrol and food coupons. They just show us where to sign and they decide upon their signatures at a later date. Keith addressed Mike and I directly: "inside of us Irish is a judge who so far has remained silent and, in any event, has no intentions of sentencing us until we deem it's our last breath. The only recriminations Kenneth and I have at the present time are those which we have imposed upon ourselves; for selling Ireland out with the same gold we've been rewarded with!"

A dark sadness spread across Siobhan's face. "Kenneth and Keith were raised in the same venomous community.

It was the quietest in the dell and we would oftentimes write flowery verse together". I remember the boys commenting that 'conflict' was the better part of verse. We both possessed such great and simple conceptions of life in those days and yet, nevertheless, we always preserved an equilibrium of sorts.

An MI6 man with a rifle looks leisurely through his binoculars from the roof of a building overlooking Grafton Street; whilst our boys rob the Allied Irish Bank's branch of £67,000. Perhaps all a stunt designed to discredit the IRA? The IRA, on the other hand, have an exceedingly dexterous double agent in the secret intelligence service – and so life keeps turning around and around on every side!

NEWSFLASH

The Provisional IRA carried out bombing outside the Old Bailey courthouse – it was March 8th 1968.

I guess that headline is what clinched things for the three of us. It was almost as though our passive action had somehow involved us in their continuous action, whilst we were doing absolutely nothing at all.

Writing poetry in the dell, zig-zagging between wearing a white or black hat was all very laudable taken at face value. However, constituting being murderous son of bitches was indeed a significant step out of line for us small town folk. On this occasion Siobhan was way ahead of Mike and I. She had quietly arranged for a minicab to take us to the station and the three of us caught the night train to Southampton.

We figured that Canada might not be a bad place to call home particularly because Mom and Dad were there. And so, the upshot was a berth for three on the RMS Franconia – its maiden voyage too. We befriended a couple of regular nice guys on board; Toni Astingura and Logan Crawford, they were heading to Toronto. We were obliged to tell them that Siobhan was our older sister because of the cabin share thing and the fact that we were a noticeably affectionate and knowing threesome!

Part 3

WHOA OH-OH, CANADA

"The Canadian is often a baffled man, because he feels different from his British kindred and his American neighbours; sharply refuses to be lumped together with either of them, yet cannot make plain this difference."

J. B. Priestley

We three; Siobhan, Mike and I, began to feel we were home two ticks after the illustrious Franconia commenced her final leg into and up the St Lawrence seaway. The gate to Canada so immense as to confuse the mind of small fry like us. Even at Rivière du Loup – a long way from its mouth – the formidable river is still 15 miles or more wide! 300 miles or so upstream at Montreal, its surpassing a mile and a quarter from shore to shore! Quebec is, of course, French and, therefore, predominantly Catholic. I guess in that respect Siobhan had an individual predilection. Mike and I were mostly schooled Protestant, yet there can arrive an on-the-spot occurrence in a person's life when all of that Bible baloney suddenly strikes a reliable chord. When a sinner abandons their shameless blasphemy, if only momentarily. We didn't meet God that evening but that is not to say we didn't touch or that we didn't pass by close. There, on the far side of the river, the sun was setting to such a delimiting intensity of heavenliness that some passengers were kneeling on the gnarled deck and praying, transfixed. It was our Mike who unpredictably remarked: "we've just witnessed God on that hill!"

The captain had decided to keep blasting the hooter and several relevant tug boats had begun to fire their hoses into the air. This was indeed 'our' maiden voyage; mute and mesmerised we inhaled the evening and hugged like we knew there would never be another to compliment it.

Quebec: the most lively, stubborn, unenlightened yet articulate Provence.

Ricky Dale 1972

Madame de Pompadour, 1759, on being told of the fall of Quebec ... it makes little difference; Quebec is only useful to provide me with furs!

Montreal seemed to have miles and miles of docks, so furiously vibrant in the early Spring when we arrived, yet all closed down in Winter when the river freezes – sometimes three feet thick! It wasn't until we were feeling pitifully peckish that we discovered Siobhan had another string to her bow – she was bilingual and spoke French fluently. Although predominantly raised in Freetown, Sierra Leone, the ambitions of the French in West Africa were almost as formidable and gluttonous as the British! Siobhan was always way ahead of us and it didn't take her long to find us all a small inexpensive bistro near the Boulevard St Laurent which bisects the city into East (mainly French) and West (largely English).

It's interesting to consider the status quo in which so few English Montrealers learn to speak French properly. And the French become (rightly so) eternally exasperated because it is always they (by the brute force of economics) who are required to become 'beautifully' bilingual. However, there is a somewhat weird kind of convention about language when heartily enjoying La Crêperie (pancakes); which everyone accepts and practices!

Now, you may be asking yourself, what about French cuisine? Well, what about it? You want French cuisine, go to France. In Montreal Quebec, they don't eat snails and frou-frou entrées. In Montreal Quebec they guzzle spruce beer and wolf down steamed hot dogs. Indeed 'steamés' as these hot dogs are known, are the national food of Quebec. If the Quebec School of Culinary Arts ever chose an emblem, it would be a hand holding a steamed hot dog proudly in the air, like a beacon, like a sword! However, curried shrimp seemed to be the 'special' today. It was really quite surreal – in a strange sort of way, nigh on like a dream; watching the men and women bent over their coffee and such, deep in conversation. Almost as if they were plotting the counter-revolution in almost any European country; who knows, perhaps they were! I guess that it was more than likely that some Anglo-Catholic-Irish baloney had gotten my imagination working overtime!

Montrealers have multiple personalities and enjoy them. Perhaps that's why us three were going to be fitting in seriously well. For example, there is nothing you can't discuss in Montreal when it comes to sex. You could call up a stranger and say, "Hi! We're taking a survey and we want to talk to you about sex! Do you like sex? How much do you like sex? How often do you have sex?" However, whatever you do, do not talk about 'love'; that really does make Montrealers uncomfortable! A typical illustration is the apartment we found in the neighbourhood north of Westmount. It was what the realtor called a "3½", meaning one bedroom with a kitchen and living room. We wrangled over the size of the bedroom and its suitability for three people to which he replied "so don't be shy!"

If it's true that men and women don't chase prospective partners who, in any way, resemble a previous partner, then perplexed as it may be, that's the reason us three hit it off both visual and desirability wise. In the most fundamental respect, we three add new elements to an age-old tradition and unfussily bastardise it!

The thing that brought us together were our idiosyncratic 'traits' – not necessarily because we were afflicted by them but, moreover, they entertained us! They not only made us more compassionate toward each other but, in Siobhan's case, they convinced her to be 'giving' in both a practical and spiritual way. She remarked that it was like being connected to the Blessed Trinity! I guess, in many respects, we owe an indebtedness to those preceding lovers whose primitive and starchy attitudes amounted to our successfulness, to wit …

My one-time partner enjoyed reproductive sex. "To procreate gives pleasure to the Lord" was her adage!

Siobhan's husband: "An equestrian by nature, astride his horse not moi!" she commented.

And as for our Mike: "She enjoyed reminding me that she was my Aunt Laura and in a heated moment would add "don't let anyone ever tell you that Henry isn't your Dad"!"

Mom and Dad had established a modest calendar month support fund to enable Mike and me in the period were on our own. Until a notification from the Royal Bank of Canada advised us it had been terminated. By all accounts Dad had been killed in a logging incident at a lumber camp. Apparently, it happened during a survey of the tundra. We subsequently learned that Mom had died from a kind of cancer not normally found in women till they begin to smoke heavily. I always imagined that Mom would have made an excellent candidate for Alcoholics Anonymous – at least she enjoyed her regular tipple until the end!

I guess that we all owe debts to individuals that we can never pay off properly – for kindness, thoughtfulness, and just plain caring – not to mention the hours of honest fun we've spent together. It is all of these and more that we owe to our Mom and Dad; and the fact that they allowed us our total independence and become who we are today.

For the first time ever, we were on Christian name terms with the clerks at the Unemployment Insurance Office, in spite of the fact that our Siobhan insisted that her big shot politician, ex-husband paid her a substantive nutriment!

It's Winter again, deep snow, cold winds off the river, fires in fireplaces aglow, red noses and sliding feet! In our house, hot rums and our Winter treat: 'Siobhan'. During the Autumn things had begun to look up for the three of us. Siobhan had found a residency as cocktail stewardess at the deluxe Ritz-Carlton. It kind of suited her plummy nature – mixing with elite upper-class folk and, of course, looking highly desirable too. Sunday won't ever be the same again because her work itinerary insisted she be on duty – evidently swanky folk are more celebratory on Sundays! However, Mondays to Saturdays we shared and dared to learn about each other so that we became, and remain, 'we', instead of just you or me!

Mike and I found a new career too; we became latter-day 'Everlys'! Having been raised in nothing much to do Nigeria, we had both self-taught ourselves how to respectably perform on a guitar. We had become almost overnight popular at indoor and outdoor ice-skating establishments across the city. We were gigging seven nights without a break, as many as four appearances per venue. On more than one occasion we were obliged to cancel because the inside of our throats had become like raw meat. Dear Mike lost his voice completely during a ten-day gig we spent singing only, with a five-piece rock and roll band. If any blame be assigned it should be to me. Dear Mike was not really a singer per se; however, he was a very fine guitarist indeed!

When we lived in Nigeria us kids had led a somewhat sheltered life. There were occasionally instances when some cause for concern was justified but, by and large, life was idyllic. Dengue and malaria were almost a yearly event, but I guess so is catching influenza in the UK. Mike had the misfortune of falling down a steep bank into a crocodile teeming creek and we once found a green mamba curled up asleep under our freestanding bath tub – the house boys grabbed it by the tail, smacked its head on the concrete floor and chopped it up for their evening meal! In spite of all of that we never once had any anxiety regarding dealing with 'human' predators, particularly of the sexual type.

Part 4

'HOW SO!'

The larger part of the Europeans with school age children settled on leaving their offspring in boarding school during term time. Mom and Dad didn't! Although our education suffered somewhat, I don't imagine that Mike and I were PhD material in any event! Mom explained it quickly and succinctly to us thus: "There are lots of poofs and bullies in boarding schools and your Dad and I didn't want you kids getting buggered or beat up!"

As it happens, our Montreal agent Emil Scharper is a 'homo' feller. He keeps very stum about it, however I oftentimes become inquisitive and want to ask him 'what's it like?' Folks in our office are really rude and refer to him as being 'gay'. It seems to me that's an incredibly inappropriate expression, inasmuch what can be gay about not having a chick to cuddle up with!

When mentioned, Siobhan reprehends Mike and I, saying that the question regarding Emil is too offensive to broach. Mike, however, draws a comparison with how inwardly our hero Douglas Bader must have felt without his legs!

It seems to us (Mike and I) that these homo (gay) folk merely have a unique predilection toward another person of their own particular intensity. Any other assumption is insensitive twaddle! Perhaps they are just prisoners of love, Mike replied. When you are a prisoner of love nothing else matters, you don't even think about escape or the consequences. As a matter of fact, you sort of hope there is no way out!

I guess some folks might consider it unusual that we have an open relationship with our Siobhan and yet we still date other folk occasionally. Sure, we have straightforward enjoyment but not all at the same time – that would be too high a price to expect from friendship.

I guess that each one of us changes day by day and what we think today might be different from what we might have thought yesterday. Last year's thoughts of our lives were right for us at that time. The thoughts we have tonight are what's right for us today. None of us are jealous and, although we both love Siobhan and we don't intend to make unloving mistakes, like regular couple often do. It seems to me that most conventional relationships are based around a love/hate intuitive. Not so with us: we pig ourselves out at that given moment and, in every respect, it's more intensive than being on a regular date – and it's always designed for a particular purpose; today or any day!

It used to bother me what others might think if they were to find out. I would just sock it to 'em, point blank: we have reliability, consistency and also a passionate compatibility, in or out of our bed! It means doing without being asked, at times without even thinking. We are a fraternity of friends and our byword is 'GIVING'!

I had a gruesome dream the other night where I shared our secret with another random lover – she said goodbye to me real quick!

Apart Together
Dearest Siobhan:
We cannot be your mind
Nor do we wish you to be ours
In loving the way we do
We must stand apart
And yet be one – us three
Using understanding
As the force that will
Keep us separated
And yet,
Forever together

Part 5

THE SUMMER OF '69

We'd spend our days loving, working and eating when we were hungry – not when told to by a clock or the sun's shadow. Oftentimes, just before dark, we'd go for a walk to one of the numerous lakes and stop, every once in a while, to wet our hands and face in the cool water. We'd walk and walk until it grew dark, and then on we'd go home, holding each other's hands; sometimes not bothering to talk – there was need because we loved, we were as one.

In the Summer of '69, it was as though the younger generation of Montrealers had been cleft in two. Those who had attended the Woodstock Music and Art Fair (or claimed they had) in one camp, and those who chose to miss it in the other. We had intended to join the revolutionary set, until a friend of Mike's called to say they stuck in mud more than a mile from the stage – moreover, they'd run short of toilet paper. One of my female playmates claimed afterwards that she had a good time after she had resigned herself to the fact that all escape routes had closed behind her! I guess that Jimi

Hendrix's rendition of 'The Star-Spangled Banner' takes on a whole new perspective if you are laid stoned in the mud! I say to all those heroes that turned up 'vive la difference' and to persuade them that there is no substitute worth its weight to strolling around Montreal at night. The streets are a buzz of activity seldom encountered by this homeboy. Cabarets, dinner theatres, clubs and bars provide a plethora of avenues for both our work and pleasure too – without having to resort to United States cow fields!

We were becoming quite well known and popular too among Montreal's Jewish community – Bar mitzvahs and wedding ceremonies were extremely good bread and butter standbys. Through all of the curves and switchbacks of our somewhat divergent past, fate had brought us here to Montreal and given us resolution.

It was Sunday and the sun concealed its glare behind our drapes. The afternoon lay ahead like another lifetime in paradise. The worldly-wise apartment and the silent street outside seemed to give credence to the view that this was indeed God's day. On early mornings like these we enjoyed sauntering through the park together, and as soon as Siobhan had finished her ablutions, that was our intention. She had changed her pink house coat for jeans and a denim shirt, glancing at herself in the large landing mirror. She had a predilection for checking out her bum and remembering her birthday next month as well.

Mike was always dressed and ready first. He resembled an Indian brave who had just emerged from Rosebud or Wounded Knee. His long straight hair drifted about two-thirds down his back and he wore his 'mandatory' silver paraphernalia around his neck and wrists like a majestic nobleman. Me, I was wearing a black turtle-neck sweater and wondering why I was so hot!

It was always a fun ride getting dressed together and if sin existed between us, it was indeed an in-depth sin, equally shared. Siobhan pulling her denims up on the thighs of her slim brown legs was a highly regarded part of belonging!

When tomorrow comes – another day, yes – but the meaning in 'I love you' will be the same as today.

Part 6

SKEDADDLE SKIDOO!

The Grand Café on Rue-St-Denis had always been a favourite of ours – live jazz, reasonable prices, and it opened early at 5pm. Oftentimes I remember thinking that if our world were to carry on like it has been thus far, we would have no need for heaven – we have it right here in our hands. In hindsight our reality – since we knew no other – was mistakenly inaccurate. It was exclusively a tricked reality – not unlike a foetus having pipe dreams when it cannot possibly know what's what, and what awaits them!

Siobhan, in contrast to Mike and my straightforward life was shared between her kinsfolk and a morose leukaemia of worry that grew and grew without mercy, doubt or even a shiver of semblance. The bizarre thing is that she had wondered into her frightened world, afraid to broach the matter with us. And now, even though unprepared for her formal confession, Mike and I were certain that the devil himself would be less demanding on what we had in mind for those who had recroched upon our Siobhan's sanity, if indeed they had? Everything we swept before us that afternoon – it was as though we were ready for it. We were certain that whatever difficulties were to ensue of the truth being told, it was better by far than not knowing.

We knew love
By its first name
And living by its last.

We were unafraid
Of what's upcoming
Or what's gone before

Knowing there's nothing left
To know or learn
Is as valuable and friendly

As the darkness once was –
Or so we thought

Siobhan spelled it out: "I owe you an explanation" she struggled. "Whether you be popes, preachers, politicians, men of prejudice or of phoney pride, when Ireland gestures your heart to return home its choice is not your choice. Whilst you may travel to foreign lands, your country of constituency will always be the intuitive isle of Ireland. It's tugging me back boys, I want to mingle with my forefathers and recapture my childhood, and sing along with my sisters (Cara and Riona) who I haven't seen for over a decade. I know you boys could easily put the screws on me to remain here with you, and it wouldn't take much for me to have a change of heart – however, please let me go boys – I will be back!"

And then Siobhan and her small red suitcase were gone – we were still drinking the wine we had opened – but she was gone. Dorval International and Siobhan had an appointment with destiny.

We didn't really realise until a moment ago, just how caught we have been in the undertone of her appeal and allure. Already an inky starless gloom had fallen over Montreal – blank, grey and irremediable to its farthest reaches. We sat side-by-side on the chesterfield, transfixed and shocked. Mike gazing at me wondering what my condition was like, me wondering likewise about him! Brothers lost in a fog of our mutual biological addiction, through a pain and fear we hadn't ever experienced previously. Next day our landlady enquired if we had watched the early Christmas parade passing past our bedroom window on Cartier Street – we had missed that too!

In the privacy of our solitude, we were certain about one intensive factor; Siobhan had left behind too much of herself in our apartment. The feel, the tone, the atmosphere – the whole damned place, it just reeked of her presence. We'd need to find an uncontaminated memory free abode, and soon! It's infuriatingly odd how once the heartbreak process has kind of run its course, how hastily our intelligence can return to its near normal self. That's not to say that being in love is fanciful or fallacious, however hopefully life continues ... doesn't it?

Thinking of Siobhan

We've had Pernod at two
In the afternoon
Sitting at sidewalk cafés
Falling more and more in love
With Montreal
And its mademoiselles
But thinking of you

We've shared sausages and bread
And our bed
With numerous dames
Not knowing their names
Or them knowing ours.
Why should they –
We were thinking of you.

Part 7

NEW RULES FOR OLD GAMES

In the quiet and melancholy cobbled streets of old Montreal we had, oftentimes, been drawn to an atmospheric bust-up property. It was obvious that someone had made efforts to restore it but most likely had run short of cash. We arranged to meet our realtor there, on the possibility that we could work some sort of deal out. The interior was in proportion to the exterior. There was a four-foot rubble wall which had collapsed into the kitchen, electrical wires going north-east to nowhere and, amongst everything else, the stink of paraffin. Since Siobhan had 'abandoned' us, we felt as though our emotional family life was under fire from all quarters. We desired a 'treat' and this house was it! Our inheritance endowment from Mom and Dad was beginning to have petered and so this rangy investment could be our last chance. In any event we have been living like tinkers and haven't had a kosher home since our bungalow in Ibadan. We figured that with a stroke of luck we could make this sows ear liveable before Winter arrives proper – that was our determined plan!

I recall mentioning our Montreal agent Emil Scharper – quote unquote "one of those homo fellers". Just last year we gave him the address of our friend Gabrial – who still occupies our former bungalow in Ibadan. Gabrial is a lad geezer too; which hit the limelight after he dared to proposition Christopher and received a slosh in return. However, Emil and Gabrial have been enthusiastically exchanging letters and Emil has offered to sponsor Gabrial through the immigration process. Mike and I have acted as guarantors too.

Although no one could become our dear Siobhan's surrogate, at the very least Gabrial is our family, and we are real eager to see him again in the new year.

My friend it's not a question
of being able to lend a hand
it's 'GIVING',
being a friend

Mike and I had already decided to give Gabrial a bedroom which, although at basement level, had its own entrance to a small garden and street. But, into the bargain, we had unquestionably agreed to create a copycat room of a concept which had impressed us both on the SS Calabar.

It was just prior to Siobhan coming on board to join us at Sierra Leone that we discovered it. Our earliest playmate of mystique and gratification. Viz: The Calabar Smoking Room. Very few passengers frequented it, especially the ladies. It was one of those throwbacks from colonisation days when the men would oftentimes take themselves off to their own little esoteric world. One of those places where, once you had experienced its splendour, it becomes sadly missed.

Dimensionally, it was similar to an average British sitting room; without rugs though. The style was somewhat rococo, although there was an excessively busy use of mahogany and louvred areas. The cushions I suspect were horsehair stuffed.

By the porthole was a compact bar with a selection of spirits in optics and free-standing; to help yourself too. From time to time, we were greeted by a steward who would bring in a small tray of willow cups and saucers and a large percolator of richly aromatic coffee. On a large round table, in the centre of the room, was an abundance of fruits and nuts and a selection of cigars and cigarillos too.

We heard from Emil that Gabrial is due to arrive at Dorval International next Tuesday. Hope he's been warned to bring warm layers of clothing as well as hats, gloves and boots!

Bar-rooms
Bed rooms
Living rooms
Dining rooms
Pool rooms
School rooms
Motel rooms
Hotel rooms

Waiting rooms
State rooms
Board rooms
Whores' rooms

We've seen them all
Lived in them too
At one time or another

If you were to ask which did you prefer, we'd have to say …

"The Smoking Room!"

Part 8

WOMEN ARE FROM VENUS!

"Hey Mike we gotta visitor – big black Merc just parked up on our slipway"

"Girls" says Mike – "they've all gone wild since Emil put us on that current EP chart."

"Seems to me" he adds "that every young woman past puberty is running around with a mattress on her back, on account she fears she's gonna miss something"

I butt in "Either that or they are agitating for liberation, which most of them already have!"

"I guess we both pine for Siobhan – you do, don't you Mike!"

"Yea, we both do my brother" he replied sadly.

"A year has passed by and not a word" I recounted.

"At first it was similar to owning a new cherry-red Ford Mustang – having her around was sort of a boyish endeavour" Mike added.

"Yea and by the time we realised we'd forgotten to roll up the windows it was too late – the water was coming in fast!" I laboriously replied.

"We have always got dear Jack Kennedy as our

exemplifier Mike – hey, his nepotisms were almost always in favour of blacks, jews and gays."

"What for heaven's sake has that got to do with anything?" I questioned.

Mike grinned broadly at me: "We've got our own in-house pair; Gabrial and Emil"

"And Jack adored the writings of S. J. Perelman and the folk poems of the great Leonard Cohen too!" says me.

Dedicatee: Siobhan

The secret way you press my hand
To let me know you understand
The wind and rain upon your face
The breathless world of your embrace
Your little laugh and half-surprise
The starlight gleaming in your eyes
Remembering all those little things
All of a sudden my heart sings
The way you dance and hold me tight
The way you kiss and say "goodnight"
The crazy things we'd say and do
The fun it is to be with you
The magic thrill that's in your touch
Oh, darling, love you so much.
Remembering all those little things
All of a sudden my heart sings

Part 9

MEN ARE FROM WEST AFRICA

When Emil and Gabrial finally met in person at Dorval International airport, it was a meeting of the 'differences' – appearance-wise that is!

Emil wore a beanie on the back of his head in the best – that is, pious – Jewish fashion. He was dressed rather nattily, I thought, in a Ralph Lauren tweedy outfit and peeping through rather thick glasses. On the other hand, Gabrial looked as though he would be more at home on a hockey rink. He was an Al Pacino type but with acne scars!

They were both 'smile a lot' people that was plain to see and, after all our essential hugs, Mike and I left them to be on their own. Before we left Emil asked us: "can you tell me whether I am in his dream or he is in mine?" Mike laughed: "Let's just say two dreams are intersecting for the moment. However, we are on your cases big time!"

The pair of them settled onto a bench where they could look out over the city. "So here we are" Emil smiled. "Yea, trapped in a dream" Gabrial replied. Emil gave a warm hand clasp: "The seriality of time has collapsed and here we are where we should be!"

"I AM NOT I"

I am not I.
I am this one
Walking beside me
Whom I do not see.

Whom at other times
I manage to visit,
And whom at other times
I forget.

Who remains calm and silent
While I talk,
And forgives gentle,
When I hate.

Who walks where
I am not,
Who will remain standing
When I die.

Juan Ramón Jiménez

There was no question that we are not happy here in Montreal. Although it was our 'adopted' home, nevertheless we had become hooked on its dubious charm. It offers to us a gentle way of life – one of the rare cities that has this exceptional ability. However, it was the 'miss you' times knowing she was far across the Atlantic that, from time to time, made us feel like 'foreigners' – kind of trapped in another country without the language of her love.

'Alchemy', a tricky word to give clarity to. Perhaps because it can mean different things to different people? It seems to me that 'alchemy' per se expresses the true conviction that 'quinta essentia' can be discovered in matter from everything that has life – provided it is refined into its highest purity. Mind and body, love and hate, good and evil, life and death, death and rebirth. It begins and ends with the transformation of the human personality – the point when the imagination guides the alchemist toward the truth. Perhaps the ultimate goal is to somehow reunite matter and spirit and thereby creating an elixir of life, through perseverance and stamina?

Part 10

'HOME FROM THE HILL'

It was as though Clarence our guardian angel had shown up that evening ... They promised him wings, so what alternative did he have but to seek out and go get Siobhan for us!

I stared transfixed out of the small mullioned window watching the clouds shifting through the evening sky and invading the ominous twilight. In my mind's eye I could see her clearly prancing along the sidewalk in that pink and beige dress she liked to wear. Sleek flaxen hair swishing and brushing her slim shoulders, arms swinging – each and every movement like a synchronous pendulum. As she rounded the corner to home, in my tormented mind's eye I missed her already; though I missed her oftentimes the same.

Mike had put on GI Blues – he never tired of the Jordanaires counting off "hut-two-three-four", However, it was a melancholy evening, and he just lay atop of her futon – the one with the daisy sheets – gazing up at the brand-new fitted skylight and beyond to the dark sky.

Have you not noticed that when a soul is almost at the point of giving up an old scratchy voice from inside them:

"Waddya really want?" That, my friend, is 'alchemy'!

The lounge door swung lazily open as if pushed by some divine being who wished to remain unannounced. "You kids still not locking-up at night – I could have been a robber." Siobhan never had an awkwardness to situations that Ms Average might have! It was as though she had filled the entrance door with angel dust – at least that's what it felt like! A diminutive gawky child held firmly to Siobhan's hand and kind of half-heartedly gave Mike and I a courteous smile. "Isn't she beautiful" Siobhan proclaimed proudly. "This is your nice new home Lisa Beth – guys; say hello to your daughter!" Without a pause she added: "we're dying of hunger, haven't eaten a decent meal since we left Dublin, 'our' child needs some meat on her bones!"

"It is you, isn't it?" Mike enquired as though he still needed a divine confirmation. "You are such a strikingly handsome woman Siobhan; I feel ashamed that we ever let you go; sorry!" "You boys weren't to know that I had swallowed a watermelon seed, but us Irish women always suffer our affliction with great dignity.

And so the evening just flew by, it was as though the pause in our lives had never taken place. We had food and beer sent over from Matty's Restaurant and Bar; Mike showed Lisa Beth some magic tricks and I read her bedtime stories. The beginning of a north-westerly was plain to hear whizzing around the house, but what did we care!

"I was three months pregnant when I left Montreal – perhaps that was sloppy of me but I dearly wanted Lisa

Beth from the outset?" Siobhan had a natural honesty and gritty elegance that was hardwired in her; however, it could be too straightforward for others to understand sometimes. "This suit I am wearing, I bought it here in Montreal about three years ago. I've got my size back, wouldn't you agree? Want to see me walk around naked or what – of course you do!"

"Worked in a piano bar – they liked me too". Mike smiled: "You at the piano with your dark specs and spot focused on you – very impressive indeed – why did you leave?"

"One night when I was tinkling the keys Lisa Beth decided to make her appearance immediately. It caused pandemonium, me splayed out on the buffet bar floor surrounded by fraught staff and vacant-headed spectators."

"They didn't invite me back after Lisa Beth was born – not because I nobbled their custom and stained the carpet. It was purely because I refused to not only play the piano but also to sing."

"I play the piano especially good on its own, but I play it really badly when I sing at the same time. It seems to be that I have a problem with playing in the same key as I sing in!"

"Enough about me; what have you fellas been up to whilst I was gone?"

"Mike and I have been thoroughly pissed off without you Siobhan."

"Ditto boys, ditto" she sadly replied.

Thread

If I love you both
Your lives instantly become
More fragile than my own,
Your body more frail
Each cough or minor pain
A symptom of some dread
Disease or other.

Death is on every road
Or in every other car
Some nights my skin
Flutters in apprehension
And I am so threatened that
Caring translates itself
Inside my head to
Stone cold anger.

Because I am insufficient
Tormented by the frailty
Of you whom I love.
Selfish I
Find you
Necessary for my own definition
Yours lives are a single thread
It snaps
I wither.

Siobhan

Part 11

LISA BETH

She loved the light in her momma's kitchen. The yellow stained leaded light panes across the top of the windows, buttered the room in a soft gold. "Your daddies have had to leave early this morning to attend a wedding ceremony in Toronto – the mayoress is tying the knot!" Siobhan felt compelled to hug their love child "they said to let you know they'll be home with us on Sunday afternoon and to bake apple tarts for supper – looks as though we've got our work cut out Lisa Beth!"

Siobhan raised an eyebrow and smiled: "You gonna tell momma how your first day of school was, or am I gonna have to make a guess?" ... "You gonna have to guess mama!" she cheekily replied.

The honest truth was that Lisa Beth was momma's girl through and through. She not only adored her Mom, but even in her child's way she knew that her momma was someone to be proud of. A friend of the family had remarked that it was as though Lisa Beth and her Mom had a kind of 'romantic' attachment.

However, with regard to her daddies, Mike and Ricky,

she just emotionally hung on their every word and vice versa. She specifically enjoyed her Dad's singing George Gershwin's "Summertime", especially when they goofed around emulating the Janis Joplin interpretation (1969). She would oftentimes sing along to the lyrics: "Your daddies are rich and your momma's good-looking". She absolutely hated the Percy Sledge song that insists: "When a man loves a woman". She said it was a stupid choice to love only one man. "Why do folks all feel the need to be exactly alike – two's better than one!"

Love is in the eye of the beholder – and likewise is life and truth

--------- The End ---------

(For now!)

Ode to Lisa Beth

A circle is my love, and all
My words along that line will tell
The radius my passions fill

You lie within it. Gently there
You nestle in its humming care,
Until its humming fills your ear

Yes, I, who spin around you, make
A universe beyond the lake,
The silent lake which is your heart.

Its depth I am, circumference round,
And moving ripples when your hand
Leans out to touch me on the ground.

And yet, and yet, it is, my dear,
Your stillness, not my turning here,
That makes the circle true entire.

Siobhan

ADDENDUM

Five memorable years have passed and we've all passed a lot of wine and cream soda since it all began. That said, if I were to drop dead right now, I'd still be the happiest guy alive (or dead!). My oxymoron is simple and profound – it's because 'ménage à trois' has produced a phenomenal gift for us all; namely, Lisa Beth.

Some critics of my work remarked "Ricky Dale's 'Siobhan's Bitches' is little more than a 'magnificent hodgepodge' – it's a 'mediocre hodgepodge'. However, thanks to the intervention of Lisa Beth, it isn't and cannot be.

Well, I trust that you have read the novel and seen for yourself why you shouldn't have read it. Or maybe on a more charitable note you may decide to read again the parts you shouldn't have read again! However, God makes stars – I merely write about them and, as celestial superstars go, Lisa Beth is one of them. And on the subject of critics: don't even give them the satisfaction of ignoring them – when we want their opinion, we will give it to them!

'SNAPSHOTS'

Taken at Siobhan's Montreal home,
just before Church

The 'brothers' enjoying a respite during a gig at L'Air du Temps

The 'divinely' sassy Lisa Beth

About the Author

Ricky Dale is a former singer and lyric writer. Although recognised as a gifted wordsmith in his adopted Canada, when he finally returned to the UK, he was virtually unknown. His revival received a kickstart after he diversified by writing novels – this is his seventh. Ricky lives in a rambling maisonette on the coast, near the picturesque town of Torquay.

https://rickydaleauthor.wordpress.com

LIMBERLOST
RICKY DALE

LIMBERLOST II
THE LEGACY
RICKY DALE

LIMBERLOST III
THE PREQUEL
RICKY DALE

RICKY DALE'S
CLOUDBURST

RICKY DALE
I KNEW
THE BRIDE
WHEN SHE USED TO
ROCK 'N' ROLL
A Ghost Story
Based on true events

THE HOUSE
ON
DUNDAS AND VINE
RICKY DALE

Also by Ricky Dale

Limberlost
A semi-biographical account of famous soprano Krystyna Comanescu, a virtuoso who has fallen from favour and seeks to bring her austere demons to rest.

Limberlost II The Legacy
This book is the captivating sequel to *Limberlost*; in which secrets galore are let slip and the truth is exquisitely unearthed.

Limberlost III The Prequel
The prequel to *Limberlost*, and a most profoundly in-depth telling of not only how it all began, but the why and the who as well.

Cloudburst
An extremely personal insight into the fact-based account of why lovers Dahlia Carriera and Sandra Comanescu choose murder as a way of life.

I Knew The Bride When She Used To Rock 'n' Roll
A charming and emotional spooky tale, based on true happenings, which has been described as "Poltergeist meets the The Sixth Sense".

The House On Dundas And Vine
A beautifully haunting story about very powerful love between ordinary people doing extraordinary things in a quite ordinary way. Essentially a true story.

Milton Keynes UK
Ingram Content Group UK Ltd.
UKHW040620090823
426573UK00001B/19

9 781787 920163